The Coin Cold Heart

Patrick John Brayer

BAMBOO DART PRESS

LOS ANGELES † NEW YORK † LONDON † MELBOURNE

The Coin Cold Heart by Patrick John Brayer

978-1-962316-17-0   Paperback
978-1-962316-18-7   Ebook

First Printing 2025

Front cover and author photograph by Patrick John Brayer

Painting by Roy Ruiz Clayton

Back cover photograph by Chris Darrow

Layout and design by Mark Givens

This is chapter thirty-one of the unpublished *The Fonta Files*

For information:

Bamboo Dart Press

chapbooks@bamboodartpress.com

Bamboo Dart Press 057

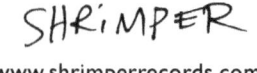

www.pelekinesis.com   www.bamboodartpress.com   www.shrimperrecords.com

The Coin Cold Heart

Patrick John Brayer

ROY RUIZ CLAYTON

Contents

Foreword

Knowing believes before believing remembers.
—William Faulkner (Joe Christmas, Light in August*)*

If it weren't for the gifts of instability I wouldn't have this ramp, nor life's molten knife-gash which leads, in its telling, to me, the story's owner. For years and years, life has been a circus tent that our ancestors erected for us, wobbly, sounding out the visible grunts, the scent of witch hazel, mule-ish, due to the greasepaint of lineage. How does one differentiate between true thought in the cottonwoods and mere cranial chatter? We examine what we say, but are never sure whether we are creating original thought. Or, are they the voicing of another within, an inner stowaway? Sometimes it's necessary to gravitate towards "the other," head-on, as estrangement without rules. Face it, thought has a voice best barked, and there, in view, glistening with it on the bedside table like an ad, gathering notice, poses a lantern-lit whisky sour. Being an artist requires accepting the voices, ones that once-upon-a-time well got a feller incarcerated. All things will come, as sure as the sky parades in Rembrandt-silver and you read the clouds as a book opening to diaphanous script. There under the vapored light, you and the unknown embrace until time has its way in the form of the Santa Anas, flinging our names like freckles of funeral ash.

Down a corridor as damp as an oyster, an alcoholic screech of tire is absorbed and spelled out in a pile of broken boxes seeming as to fabricate, or rather surmount a rendition of The Last Supper in cardboard. You watch the way people live and you can't help but slap down on a mosquito, splat, and rear back in wonder at it, as the blood-jam remains of life itself. Your heart goes out to them, enmeshed and pumping. In the manner of stirring jambalaya with a bayonet, a symposium of primitive man might feel compelled not to model anything more necessary than the present moment. The pot-hole homeless that we spy each day on the asphalt streets, at the helm of reach, yet tight rope walking the star-lit thread of a razor's edge. It turns out, they are no less than time-traveling pirates steering back from an apocalyptic future, hitching up their pants, now lost in a gutbucket experiment. A trail that just hurries through time without bothering to seek permission. So far back from the future, unfortunately, that they seemed heaved, reined in by standing still, like so many soft grapefruit, thusly beyond the grasp of accepted usefulness, as if repeating a seance over and over until one hears only the target of their needs rudely tailgating their wants. The mind somehow moves through the light-years slower than the body, so it is believed that the mental information will not meet back up with those subjects for something roughly in the range of seven galactic life spans. Give them bright shaggy slippers, accordion lessons, and oak-burning bourbon, rebooting thoughts as frail as a gull's wing at the dump, and then lace that with LSD drops, thus heading reality off in midstream. Regardless, their minds will still not get here, as if by vaunted decree, any sooner than in due time.

A finger snaps in and out of a cold-cocked dream. You and I meet here now in this story's present, introduced to each other at an outlaw biker's garden party, spontaneously held in the parking lot of the Chino State Prison for Women. We converse, and jovial wordplay comes to mind. This over the matching glint of two frostbitten vodka gimlets, somehow heavy on Everclear grain alcohol in poetic license, both of us bolt upright, spouting something to the effect of, "Let's get real, front and center, in finding this whole valley here as once the silt bottom floor of the sea." Pre-history they go to calling it. Why doesn't anyone want to take that into account? And what remaining energy at present is still of that ill-remembered time? That's what sunglasses achieve. They take us back to the vision we peripherally remember from underwater, a time before we evaporated that tell-tale dimension and parked our gills at the curbside for a wiggle onto terra firma.

Arriving at the present, greased beyond our grasping, in that million-year vehicle that we call, "our today." We are brave enough to harken it, but we are stupid to ever think it might come when we call. Notice how when you go to jump into the ocean, treadmill waves like a roll of nickels perpetually try to muscle us back onto the earth, linebacker fashion, cast from its garden of brine. To each his own, say the elements, but to themselves only. For what to one person is a comically painted sunset, a rendered attack of yellows by some blue-haired art-club grange-hall bitty, was to another an acetylene gold ray raining down upon a sparsely attended graveside. No one is alone in the casket, every person is buried with their shadows. This makes me think of the old saying, "She's got you on a short leash." Who among us is not on a short leash if you're looking for it? It's funny how it doesn't appear to exist when you're not looking for it. True to the fact that something lost is still there and that there is nothing that doesn't, in the locomotion of nothingness, tirelessly bother to exist. This only proves, after all, that the hurricane is, as they say, just the devil slamming his wife up against the heavenly gates in the troubled heart of an opera.

The Fontucky Creation Myth

At one time all the people of Fontana lived on self-fashioned boats or barges, for this was a prehistoric period in which the world was all water, and dry-earth had not yet been invented, nor mountains pushed up into eruption, yet to meet their carnal destiny with the cobalt vestment slashing shadows of the future. Scientists of today have come to discover the fallacy within the long-adored Big Bang theoretics, its galaxy turning to a floating congregation of globes, only to find that the San Gabriel Mountains were, in anthropological terms, no more than a muddy bootprint left behind by a giant, step-stoning from planet to planet on its trek across the universe. It was later known to have been distracted by a meteor, tripping on Jupiter, and banging its shin like a bloody sunset on the sharp corner of a black hole.

At first, all humans lived under the sea, but, due to the creeping evolution of morality, cheating husbands had one by one gradually become banished and sent atop the water, this by a female judge and jury, with only a handful of midnight floozies, in mistress exile, present above the salty ocean to calm them, with stark faces of thickly perfumed war-paint, flailing their sassy boas of seaweed.

Amongst the many huge barges, one held a steel mill, puffing islandesque, while another held a circus equipment junkyard. Yet another dilapidated scow held the *Sugar Shack* strip club, where hard-working men in slave's sweat could be found wandering out back into the open chill, bedazzled by the rude pleasures of femininity, into what foresaw the blueprint prototype for what would become known as the "vacant lot." This is an equivalent cold shower. There to be found, a fistful of rural charm, with the welcoming starry strung Balina courts, lively festooned behind the nightclub, throbbing like the bellows of a blacksmith, emulating until 'last call,' either rancorous fireflies or a swift kick to the head.

In a more particular time back then, there were two men out casually and rhythmically rocking on a beautiful hand-made teakwood yacht, both billowing hand-rolled kelp cigars, stereo chimneys, a hallucinatory treat of the period, their vessel situated ten thousand feet above where we find Fontana today. You could immediately tell they were good friends on account of the shared ease of demeanor and the subtle similarity in dress, as if their dead moms still dressed them from a hunting catalog now long lost in the diet of the couch cushions, and the fact that they never had to look at each other, long ago settling into a telekinetic laziness in which their speech sauntered when it spoke in a golden-hearted gunslinger's slang. This particular mention in time found them in oceanic isolation which spread, or shall we say splayed, way beyond the sight of any other such comrades.

The lapping come-hither-ness dealt out with mirage-tipped clouds overseeing, trying but never seeming quite to undo the dream they were belched out of. The one gentleman told the other, the boat's owner, that he secretly played the guitar over the years, and that it saddened him quite a bit that he did not have it at this moment, a moment in which, with it in his hands, he might be able to interpret the muse of this unforgettable light, quickly fading, one that the two of them shared there like a meal. A light particular in that it was as if every molecule in that sea air was charged to the brink of exhibitionism. The boat owner was so moved by the other's sincere desire, to the point that moisture began to lounge on the lower lip of his eyelid, both eyes quickening, steak-red, like a Catholic Sacred Heart seeing itself in the mirror. Then, as if receiving some hallucinatory order, he rushed down into the cabin below deck in a clip-clop bongo of steps. There he began to furiously chop a section out of the hull of the boat in the very shape of a guitar, which suggested to him, in a trance, to trace a woman's hips in the pace of his work.

Within an hour, using only a gooseneck bolt and some marine spikes as tools, he had pounded, carved, and strung with fishing line, a museum-quality guitar for his friend, silent yet for a smile. He stained the already dark teakwood with blood sausage and seamed its bouts with a purfling of glass shards. Such was their shade of deceptive green that it became impossible to turn from it an eye's remove. The only problem was, that in making the hole in the floor of the boat, it was now sinking, and so found itself a sad halfway submerged, and there then navigating nowhere but down into the dark limousine blue ocean, black as blue can be, and one that had now grown as ice bitten as a martini at *Musso and Frank*. As they stood on the last remaining tip of the cock-eyed vessel, the guitarist twirled down to his knees and in that instant sang a spontaneous lyric through silver teeth in a guttural livestock auctioneer's baritone. A song so beautiful and overly private that the two men's certain death was then, as if forever, overshadowed by the sound-sonnet's abstractly undebatable miracle, and for lack of a better word, celestially conjured content. The chorus concluded in its crescendo what one would assume might be the hook and title, *The Coin Cold Heart.* The song cried out verse by verse the tale of a man's unanswered love for a pig farmer's daughter who was then sidetracked, her having an affair and running off with a married merman of the ocean. It concludes with the distraught jilted man getting changed surgically into a fish so he could dive down and vengefully kill the merman, only to find out that he could, as a result of that attempt, no longer breathe *above* water, and so it appeared would never be able to see his family again, nor then his heart's access to the swine farmer's daughter. He does then finally track down a surgeon on the bottom of the ocean who agrees to change him back, but sadly only to drown on the way back up in his ill-thought-out ascension to the surface.

A Song's History

The first singing performance of the song was indeed so powerful that the two men just stood calmly, and at an escalator's pace, they were entrusted into the lower department of the sea's swallow. Fortunately, in a well-timed fate, a bird was gleefully caroming by the boat at the very moment that the man cried out his solitary version of the song. The bird, a genetic mocker, tombstone feathered, learned the song in swift passing, and in so he sang it as he went knuckle-balling through the mist, there towards another vessel that stood so far off in the distance that only an eye with mouse-catching instinct could even begin to fathom it. The duo's descent continued and finally gargled the song straight into the sea, and there in finality into the food chain of a Cuisinart of jealously colored sharks. Their final voices sounded like the bark of rags tearing as they were accepted by the sea down a circling drain, like a jellyroll maelstrom.

The bird was growing old and tired and so decided to retire from flight and settled on a large flat football field of a barge that was invested in the harvest of grapes. He would sit on the white garden fence of the vintner, and with a husky tone of purpose, he daily sang in a savant's repetitive dedicationalism, the titanic depth of the acquired song. All was a greasy powder blue perfect, until one violently lazy day in a montage of flying feathers, and the scream of stolen life, wherein the man butchered and cooked the bird in the wine of his estate, plums, and a savory contortion of Chinese chilies. His teeth were squeezing the broth from the tough fowl, as he now mumbled his mind's recording of the song, to himself, to the metronome of his heavy boot on plucked feathers, that and the stubborn tambourine cadence of dreams that he had reserved for himself.

Somewhere far off and relatively deep there was the faint sound of a shark burping up a coat pocket, and a hand-carved guitar floated thousands of feet above what today is "*Woody and Lena's Good Deal Shop*," a thrift store on Sierra Avenue in Fontana. The only recorded copy of the song, after a million years of secretly and mentorally changing hands, as if passing a torch of flaming dueling pistols, finding itself somehow preserved on a quarter-inch spool of brittle reel-to-reel tape, an ancient stain on modern technology, located in the very back room of that gloomy aforementioned pawn establishment. The box that housed the tape, misnamed, gave no reference to its actual true contents. According to how it read in scrawl, it was said to have once housed a compilation of Cajun Klu Klux Klan numbers by someone calling itself Johnny Rebel. The sacred song, *The Coin Cold Heart*, in its entirety, even in these modern times, had shifted hands on a plethora of spontaneous accounts before it then wound up in this Fontana impersonation of an Oklahoma hayseed serial killer's off-plumbed toolshed. There it was, so innocently tilted up against a plastic warming episode of *Oprah*, and there prey to the microscopic mites and the failing color palette of remnant shag carpeting. The version on the tape was only just accidentally recorded at an open-mike hoot night in a garage in the rock quarry burg of Pedley, California. All this before then taking on an extraterrestrial kidnapping or two. But you'd have to admit in observation that its history was vague and its secret sources not entirely to be trusted. It was lucky that the audience ignored its open mike onset because if not handling its content carefully, upon concentrating on the substance of the song, it is warned that one will either reach bliss-enhanced enlightenment or become the product of an audio 'ordeal poisoning' in a permanent horizontal form. So in time, the history of its transference had somehow come to be placed under the protection of a locally based religious cult, a nameless one that ran a new-age sports bar as a front in Fontana, a steelmillion Loredo all its own. The masquerade tavern was called *The Cucamonga Wilderness,* which sported a horseshoe bar hewn from polished sinker cypress. That bellied up to a kaleidoscopic Tiffany of colored bottles banked in front of, and protecting, three original candle-lit Rothko originals of the three blurry panels variety. The bar would film and project sporting events themselves to be more from the surreal vantage point of the picture's composition than to the participants trying to conquer each other. It was always viewed in super slow motion, or tai chi speed, and backed by a loud droney ambient synthesizer soundtrack that grabbed and straightened your rib cage like one corrects his tie. There was no talking allowed in the "Wilderness" as they called it. Sometimes slurred "The Wilberness," or by its detractors, "The Wildebeest." The room was so highly soundproofed that you could hear the dust particles arguing, as then every other half-hour, for a half-hour, there would be a palette cleansing of stone silence, as the bar served freshly juiced carrots, pineapples, curly kale, and ginger root in multi-floral shell-shaped tumblers. The only alcoholic drink that they served was Japanese sake with Russian vodka, garnished with a sugar cube impaled by a bamboo spear and doused with a dose of ecstasy. Using this establishment as a front they proceeded to raise the money required to find and hide the song and the guitar successfully. If it was played out on the radio no one is quite certain how many thousands would die. Religion has always ignored that polite consideration that we should all live by: "Don't show people something that can harm them because then they can never un-hear it." That is said to be the biggest flaw in our manufacturer, that it failed to make us unable to un-see or un-hear the simplest things. That is the beauty and the wealth in the medium of silence. They attest that it is the only spiritual element that is the same when seen as when unseen. Thus making it the equalizing palindrome that makes the millionaire go down and crawl into the cardboard box with the wino, bathed in raw moonlight, and help stir his sparrow soup tincture for him with his watch, pinky extended, taking tiny sips together like the queen's court. A Rolex tea, you might call it. According to the *Cucamonga Wilderness* lore, only one person is allowed to have the song in their head, and if or when they show up, in the middle of the night at your house in the rain, under a sky of broken spittle, stoned at your screen door, wearing speckled tweed with a soft wolf collar, that it is evident that you are either going for the bloom of nirvana or eternal chess with the calcified soil.

Graduated shades of yellow and blue create a rug-burn of the day's end. Vaulting over with decks of light are the make-shift 'seat of the pants' churches that taunt Sierra Avenue. They looked like a sideline of sandlot players waiting nervously, yet they never got to play. Thrift store Woody tells the story one more time about his metal flake Cadillac of a burnt orange pallor, with cow horns matadorally chicken-wired onto the front grill. The near-petrified 78 rpm recording of his band, on *Nashboro Records* in the fifties, is still displayed, as the only remaining copy, cracked completely in half, rendering it unplayable. But the long lost tape still lies brewing, its box disintegrating with termites in shared housing, but the magnetic residue still holding its sleeping powers. Woody does not know about it, and the cult doesn't know where this original copy is. Only you and I know so far. There is a rumor though, that the cult members have the *covenant of the ark* hidden in Fontana somewhere beneath the *Ken-Tuk-You-Inn* on Valley Boulevard, and amongst its contents, there is falsely rumored to be, one teakwood guitar with canvas rotting straps for a capo.

We all go back to those memories of when we lived a strict nautical life, but we don't know it. For instance, our love of Doritos chips is due to our sea-faring memory of the triangular lateen sails of old, brought to a turmeric state by a bright organdy sun's fester. The way film flies from a camera like a fly-strip dangling, our true feelings, whenst exposed, will not make cloned pictures, but ones being fresh and new. To live one day of the year unclothed and back on all fours, is that too much to ask of a public holiday? Let yourself now imagine a Goddess in rose-red linen. Imagine the lime taffeta slip and white spectator pumps. A stubbled cheek rubbing against the row of coral velveteen buttons that are all that's left to remind us of the history of all time and place.

The Wilderness cult instructs us that when we die, and our skin grows nightgown pale, we are allowed to take with us only one memory. The decision has to be made. Until which we hang, with a coin cold heart, in limbo, and no one is allowed to begrieve us until we, in the clock's laminated eye, choose. However far this story stretches the Niagara Falling idea of time-passage, it equally questions in retrospect the frank indelicacies of sung speech, retiring patiently unto blushful passages, islanded on the page, to a metronome of a bare bulb swinging through sweat fog, pulling honky-tonk lust all but under the sea.

The memory of another invisible hero I will tell you about was not in fact a firsthand memory per se, but rather a memory of a dream undreamt. But they let that pass. Although it is buried and made of a million passing years, it is real. One memory comes to mind of a man with a mysterious barge, almost invisible, always surrounded by gunmetal fog which was thought from a safe distance to be illuminated by buried lightning, depth-charged voodoo pyrotechnics, as arc welding had yet to be thought up. The man here had no name, nor did anyone on the earth at this point. If a man wanted to talk to another they just walked up to them and spoke, no need for a name if you recognized someone. Here's an example: Think of your best friend. Can you picture them? Now tell me, do you see their face or do you see a nameplate? This is one of the many ways in which man has gotten lame over the cognizant millennium. The man I'm speaking of was a hermit on this floating isle and was the tribe's sole inventor. His facial demeanor housed a nose likened to a ripe cactus apple. His trembling skull was topped off and made unfriendly with a crop of bushy corkscrew locks. Don't even mention his eyes, more like staring into the mossy double-barrel soul of bilgewater than not. He didn't want visitors and less than nobody wanted to come up against him. So it was, the rare yet perfect union. A lot of his inventions had been excavated recently, buried for millions of years, in and about the North Fontana foothills. One excavation found a row of about twenty fully farm-operational tractor-driven combine harvesters, that sported single-port feeder-house latching and a mass-flow sensor. This was extra strange since gasoline hadn't even been discovered. He just simply invented what was pictured in his head. He was the last to know that it was a blueprint escaped from the future. Upon demolition, another find was found under Nealy's Corner Cafe in 1994. It was what appeared to be a fully loaded Buick Skylark with eel skin seats and a fully operational V8 engine that had never been fired up. After carbon dating was established at about three million years, they concluded that the paint was made from the concentrated pigment of melted sharkskin, a shade the old inventor liked to call, bluesome.

Part Two: Sin Coalfield

"I went to a restaurant that says it serves breakfast anytime.
So I ordered French toast during the Renaissance."
—*Steven Wright*

In the capacity of a freelance investigative journalist, I was hired to spy and acquire one missing pre-historic guitar, based upon some new promising leads, on behalf of the now notorious *Wilderness* cult. To be only as honest as I can afford to be, I needed the work, myself being on parole like most of the people I knew, but I couldn't help but see this as a 'mop-up inning' in the grueling baseball game that paraded as 'my life atoned.' From a hazy high authority, meeting secretly at the lunch counter at The Smokehouse billiard room, encircled by hard hat hair and snooker tables, I was given a map and ordered to a dilapidated property off Cherry Ave. that supported a house and scrapyard, all but spelling out in scrub remains that it was just a further part of the slapdash remnant-past, thrown upon an old steel-industry battlefield. The only thing symmetrical about the clapboard shack that anchored the view, in first impression, was a sentinel set of anorexic bushes stationed on either side of a cobalt door with an uninviting knife stabbed into it at approximately an eye's height. The bushes nervously clog danced, they marionetted in a Santa Ana wind that served up a lungful of slag dust for no extra charge. The scalp of some distant hills seemed to peek goldenly upon the scene. The house smelled ugly in the dark, fragmented glass still out in the lane where jaundice-haired street kids had shot out a streetlight utilizing their uncle's parole-hidden shotgun. A ghost of a fence bunted the front stretch of the yard, missing a good deal of the pickets, simulating a Leon Spinks smile, coming off like a prisoner that etches the numerical path to his remaining days in stir onto the cinder block wall in caveman stick figures of five. Right off I noticed a few of the excavated pre-historic Columbines half-covered in morning glory vine, yet tall enough to still hover over a tall fence collection of corrugated metal portions, probably from a buried winery gone asunder. The man who lived here was said to be one Sin Coalfield, sole occupant, known to exist off the grid, who had no social security card nor driver's license that anyone could find evidence of. What no one knew about him though was that he had attained underground fame in the early '70s for his watercolor paintings of women's sacred parts rendered in the style of his seance-muse and mentor, 17th-century botanical illustrator, Maria Sibylla Merian (1647-1717). A little-known fact is that both Jack Nicholson and Roman Polanski both had Coalfield botanical drawings tattooed blazingly on their chests.

I'm not a quality thinker but still, I used to think many things. You'd assume that you'd accrue more and more options as you grew old, but that's not true, no, you just re-thought everything in a different light. At one time I would have thought I was the polar opposite of such as Coalfield, but I grew to realize I was his reflection, of no one's making, a fancified outlaw for the sake of the law. I once entertained the life of a songwriter or a poet, but the world, in lockstep, told me differently. I used to listen to the radio and think, "Well that's awful, I should have no problem here." But over time I changed my tune, it became "My songs are just as lame as that, this should be no problem." But it *was* a problem, as romantic as it seems, me sleeping in the sun-faded back seat of a Ford Fiesta for my art, a hooded sweatshirt for a pillow, which shouted in big red letters the hunting-dog slogan *"When the tailgate drops, the bullshit stops!!!"* All this to an inviting Sterno-lit dinner of Bean and Bacon soup washed down with a resplendent sea of Jim Beam, or at least as much as I could beg afford. An ancient 8-track tape, almost the shape of a veal cutlet, wobbling the vocal cords of Buck Owens Live in Las Vegas. So eventually I got a job like everyone else, which should not for the life of things be misconstrued as reality. Although I had no backup talents, I wasn't necessarily a private detective, every ounce of Raymond Chandler's Dead Sea Scrolls of Pulp proved that. I, rather, only had the capable talent enough to do things that people could have and should have just done themselves. Everyone has a trigger of guilt, and this is mine. When I was twenty-one I had witnessed a man having a heart attack on a sidewalk in town. There was nobody else around and I had no clue what to do. So I did the only thing I was trained to do, I got out my notebook and wrote a quick poem for him, set it on his chest, and walked away. He died a few minutes later and the poem blew away just before the ambulance arrived in its 4th of July light bar display. I didn't know it then but that moment would inform the rest of my life, or at least the grand opening of a well of pity from which I would often plunge my bucket.

In attempted stealth, I hid the car behind a coin-operated vending machine that sold square-foot blocks of ice. Here I celebrated the passage of the seasons over a deck of Chesterfield coffin nails while beating a nervous tribute to Gene Krupa rhapsodically on the grime-skinned steering wheel, and waited for the sun to piss off. There was extra money in the deal, a cool million if I could retrieve the teakwood guitar, and an undisclosed extra sum if I could find the reel-to-reel recording of *The Coin Cold Heart*. Unfortunately for me, I had thought in detail more about how I would spend the money, than I did about how I might learn to earn it. Darkness had finally descended into a chokecherry nighttime. Adorned in a black ski hat which I bought for an absent interview with the merchant marines, I gravitated toward the only light, a large picture window on the frontage of the house. I come from a school that believes, all and all, that houses often have more of a spirit than the people within them. You need to approach a house with respect, even if you only intend to sell them an encyclopedic vacuum cleaner or merely systematically eradicate the inhabitants. In inspecting the house, the house inspected me right back. We were good. In a makeshift do-si-do I bellied up to its huge plate glass dinosaur's eye. The moon threw a faint lunar glove of night light in my path. Inching forward, my dragging steps rousing the rancorous smell of tumbleweed dust, I sheepishly ducked to peer into the dim molten aquarium nature of the scene. You'd want to think that this was film noir lighting, but you had to remember that the only reason that minimally lit genre existed in the first place was that *The Wizard of Oz* and all the block-buster films of those times were using all the good lights on such as Toto's profile, leaving the remaining dregs for what were then considered B movies. The curtains were pulled and seemed to have no memory of their original color and looked, in stop action, as to have been raped by the rest of the room, which consisted of a couple of eucalyptus stumps serving as chairs, and a flimsy card table. I finally got a good gander at our Sin Coalfield as I looked on in what I hoped wasn't ignorant caution. He didn't appear to be paranoid because the curtains were open to the whole wide world, yet there he was in all his ribald character. I still did think, in an attempt at professionalism, to put out my cigarette in an unemployed flower pot lest it be mistaken for a laser sight on a deer rifle. I viewed the man, soaking in the observation of his demeanor. After my mind comingled the ripeness of my own well-earned musk, after sitting in the hot car, I could easily imagine his smell being mine, a conquering feral aromatherapy, moving effortlessly through the plate glass. I observed in him a man of about sixty years of age, a forgotten russett of an individual, overweight and perspiring either from drugs, or he was a major shareholder in Little Debbie's cupcakes. His face required a good imagination to even own a mirror, the time-clawed lines in it going in unearthly directions, the course identity in his face seemingly constructed of shuffled layers of indifference. His teeth were the right color if you were digging up antiquities, to which the vacancies outnumbered the originals, as he drooled thread-like lines on a flannel bathrobe. What he held in his lap, and which hid the kilt he had on beneath the robe, was the pearl in the very center of this diorama, the teakwood guitar that I had hungrily hoped to cast my eyes upon. It was in amazing shape considering its age and now sported an electric pickup, mounted gracefully into the Edvard Munch scream of the soundhole. It was presently plugged into a well-beaten Sears and Roebuck amplifier, itself upon its last garage-band legs, tubes burn-glowing a sign of life, the cable held in place at its insertion point by a paint can. The guitar's voice was amazing with all of its string's elasticity waving at different sets of speed. His hair swung in about twenty beaded braids as he strummed the instrument, sometimes clacking percussively, resembling a maraca of teeth. The music he played was not good. Actually, it was technically awful by sub-rational standards. But there were other things one had to consider. It appeared to me then, the music critic, that he was playing as if his hands were driven out into a vineyard in a Lincoln Continental and broken by hell-bent thugs, getting in one last crime before the rapture. I later learned the truth behind the style, and that he was playing it with dead-on accuracy. The instrument was now meant to be played as if by our biological ancestors from back when our species were still in the sea. So, naturally, he was playing it as if he didn't have hands but yet only flippers. Once you understood that it was Mozart backed with the Babel-falling 'razor-blade to the speaker cone' power chords of Link Wray. Even the paint can had become profound in its wake. It all tied together for me, through deductive skills, straight in with the Rothko paintings at *The Wilderness*. Now I was getting it. They could not be addressed as paintings at all, they could only be looked into. Viewed from the outside the art was gibberish, but when looked into became a sort of cosmic freefall. The same with the teakwood music, it meant nothing that all our knowledge could help us with. It was a dimension beyond what we know as music, and that's what made it lethal when combined with the lyrics. My subject didn't look violent, just a little drunk on the music. Still, I panned the room in search of weapons that might, in the event of a tussle, shorten my life span. I found nothing but a crossbow hanging from a rusty nail. It was a modern one, not one of the King Arthur type. The newer ones just look ridiculous, probably just meant to stop you in your tracks, like a deer in headlights, you wondering why someone was coming after you with Suzanne Summer's old Thigh-Master. It's funny how everything boils down to your motivation. My talent was not that of the art of investigation, my talent was in the art of eating, or that of not starving. That's as far as it goes. So the more I thought about how I was to go about this, the more confused I got. Which led me to just bursting in the back door without a plan at all. I took off my boots at the back door-stoop and silently padded across the kitchen floor. There, although nothing could surprise me, was a naked middle-aged woman passed out on her back on the kitchen table. As I checked to see if she had a pulse I ran a gaze down her perfect body, which in this situation I was in no position to appreciate, as white as homogenized cream with a slight blue cast from the fluorescent bulb that hovered from above like an alien spacecraft. I tried not to get aroused just in case she was dead, for that would assuredly result in years of therapy, a happenstance that a person like me could ill afford. Thankfully she awoke slightly as I touched her neck for a sign of life. I put a finger to her lips in an act of silence and she fell back into tranquil slumber. I could see the back of Sin Coalfield's head from behind a beaded curtain festooned with an inviting hula girl most likely from some Honolulu Desert Storm. He rather cut a profile of menace to me now, his nose pointing around the room like a policeman's gun, which dripped with salty diamonds of sweat, making little swan dives into a ratty herringbone rug. At this point, when I had given up on figuring out what to do next, instead of on what not to do, the naked lady came from behind me holding a firearm, a policeman's special, and I thought of how life just wasn't fair with all of its endless variables. I closed my eyes and waited to die when all of a sudden she came right up to my face, dropped her gun hand to her voluptuous side and began kissing me dramatically, her lipstick surrounding my mouth appropriately rendering me a mad jester. She put the gun in my hand and wrapped my fist around it, our fists laminated together like one hand grenade, while she stepped back to straighten the auburness-hair into fish-shaped curls, her beauty was curious to me and tipped the domestic scale, while her smile came at one at the angle of playful grimace, long stolen perchance from a fairytale princess. She just stood and stared at me in a fashion that women always do when they expect you to make them a cocktail with too many components. A concoction embellished with a sword-shaped toothpick, a celery stalk, or chia seeds fermented in unicorn blood. I checked the revolver, it was loaded all the way around. I tip-toed into the living room and without ceremony shot Sin Coalfield four times in the back and he fell like a sack of turnips, just as a dead man's supposed to. His trucker-style ball cap tumbled across the floor as if blown by a ghost, reading 'Pomona Feed' on its skulled bonnet. I would ordinarily think that that was a clue or an omen, but I was beyond all that now. I then realized for the very first time that transcending and giving up are identical twins, although, as the rules go, one of them must

PATRICK JOHN BRAYER

still choose who plays the black sheep in the family. I gathered up the teakwood guitar and amplifier and made a few lumbering trips loading them into the coalmine darkness of my Ford Fiesta, the scene outside lit just barely by the bone saw teeth of the moon. I came back into the house and sat and cried in a widow's moan until sunrise, with Coalfield at my stocking feet, with the blank expression of an egg, in his bathrobe and kilt, in sort of a nautilus shape, looking, in the same manner, both absurd and regal simultaneously. The doomed nature of the scene reminded me of a story my uncle once told me regarding the true history of Saint Patrick. It seems that when he was driving all the snakes out of Ireland each one in exit got placed a potato on its back, thus putting the famous famine in gear. Outside the weather changed to hard sheets of rain, jostling the trees into the shape and surrender of desperately blind bodies clumsily dressing in the dark.

I don't know about you but I didn't know whose to blame for moral bankruptcy, mine, yours, theirs, or ours. I feel we're all the same in one respect. That is, we can't bank on mining some ethics that we can't even find. You might be an awful parent ricocheting your kids off in one harmful direction after another. You might be able to afford an analyst who then tells you what's not missing. Most people think that that is the fix, that that's enough, but it isn't. You still have to go deep inside yourself and find that missing thing and bring it back. That's what they don't teach in college, that knowing is never enough. It's never real until you find the knowing down in yourself and haul it up. It has to survive the whole trip and arrive recognizable, unruptured by the razor eyes of this wolverine-skinned rulebook we tote. I was going deep down into the depths of myself right now, a huge bunker of a space, and finding that just about everything in need was missing, even the metaphoric janitor was high on cleaning solvents. Then the mysterious woman came back in and in a motherly flourish brought me a warm enchilada plate in one hand, drowning in nasturtium flowers, and in the other some high-octane coffee served in a Waterford Chrystal cowboy boot, Johnny Cash's signature etched upon it as clear as day. It was as if all of life were one big speech impediment, attempting clarity with a mouth full of nails. I wasn't even sure if she owned any clothes, but that's the way I took her home with me that day, as en route before us the bars and churches were all slowly coming to life in an almost competitive fashion. I sold the pilfered guitar to *The Wilderness* cult as promised for a cool million. I set the woman up in her own apartment at *The Juniper Arms* in Fontana, rash-pink stucco

PATRICK JOHN BRAYER

and palm trees, just across the street from the town's only headshop eye sore. Although I never did ask nor did I receive her name, I visited her daily. I brought her supplies, as I was to find out that she was agoraphobic and was unable, or at least had no real desire to leave the apartment. She admitted to the fact that she had been raised in captivity and had never in her life worn clothes, resulting in love and cruelty becoming one and the same to her. But she was 'good people,' and did me a great favor that day we met, by not bothering to kill me. What is life anyway if not just a string of days where one doesn't get killed? Lest we forget that if we piled all the gathered shadows in the world, laid on the floor before us, they would still be devoid of substance. Not remembering where she grew up on account of trauma was a trait she wore. It was either California or Florida, one of those holster-shaped states it was once thought. I set her up with cable TV and when I'd come to visit she'd be watching old black and white movies, lost, in character, in mock dramatics, reciting the actor's lines verbatim along with, sometimes before them. Sometimes we would find ourselves watching blue movies into the night, concluding in agreement that ultimately size conveys relative significance, not reality. Other times I would sit with my eyes closed, my big lump of a head and jug ears in her lap, and just listen to the dated porn soundtrack, easily sounding of a couple writhing distraught in a fluid sack of snakes, offering up a satanically-drenched violin, sonically sawing a lonely cry from a cat-gut stretch of string.

At one point the other tenants complained of her constant state of undress, in which case I bought the whole complex, kit and caboodle, lock stock and barrel, kicking everyone else out, and had secure fences and gates installed around the peripheral edges of the property. I had a swimming pool built for her in the shape of the sacred guitar, which now that I think of it, was very similar to her own voluptuous shape, as I spy down on her now in joy, her nest on fire, humming *The Coin Cold Heart* in a mumble of notes, as she sun-worshiped on its teakwood deck.

The Coin Cold Heart

She said five frail Hail Marys
Then she broke my heart of prison bread
I held tightly to the edge of the world
Until unto oceans part the dead

All boots and pistols
The earth no less round than the eye
To the sight of only soot and salt
An Alabama do or die

Me and the pig farmer's daughter
A merman surfaces night-drenched at the dock
Our eyes race the second-hand
Long 'round the old farmhouse clock

Fifteen pounds of pursuit
Ocean field of glass
To a coin cold heart in reckoning
Here to stay we come to pass

Rotten bridle on the cold cream mare
The one with the coin cold stare..........

*(The author has left off the final lines due to the fact that if one should read the lyric in its
entirety it would mean instant death. That would be his gift to you for gettin dis' fur')*

Acknowledgments

"It's easy to corral my influences as mutual appreciating, as they start slow and plunge deep. Leaving me not able to help but feel that they collectively, just by being, tell my story better than I can."

My Posse: Chris Darrow (Claremont CA), Alison Krauss (Champagne IL), Ben Chase Harper (Benwood CA), Michael Hedges (Mendocino), Stuart Duncan (Gnashville TN), Lyle Lovett (Klein TX), Richard Stekol (Capistrano), John York (San Antonio Heights), Greg Copeland (Full Cleveland), Porter McKnight (Bamatreyu), Pat Cloud (Long Beach), Dennis Callaci (Claremont), Roy Ruiz Clayton (Louisville KY), Michael Alan Brayer (Fontandiego), Hollace Brayer (Wrongtario), Eleanore Frances Brayer (Fontana CA), Robb Strandlund (Muscoy), Dick Barnes (Mt. Poetry), Tim Weed (Petaluma CA), Rob Morrow (Northfield MN), and Jack Hardy (NY)

About the Author

Brayer was raised on an egg ranch in the steelmill town of Fontana, California. Think Hell's Angels, think Sammy Hagar, think Shelton Brooks. Developing a unique style of writing early on as an answer to his inability to speak, he went on to receive an education in music from an array of dirt parking lot honky tonks that befriended a Valley Blvd. truck route. To his own surprise his writing has led to the winning of eight Gold, Platinum, and Grammy Award winning projects. To this day he admits that he likes to write prose best because "when doing that, while managing to be unsuccessful, people leave you alone". Humble but not one prone to self-deprecation he was once heard to say, *"Hey, by hook and by crook, I'm better than I'm supposed to be."*

112 N. Harvard Ave. #65

Claremont, CA 91711

chapbooks@bamboodartpress.com

www.bamboodartpress.com